Sharing Books From Birth to Five

Welcome to Practical Parenting Books

It's never too early to introduce your child to books. It's wonderful to see your baby gazing intently at a cloth book; your toddler poring over a favourite picture; or your older child listening quietly to a story. And you are your child's favourite storyteller, so have fun together while you're reading – use silly voices, linger over the pictures and leave pauses for joining in.

In *Good Luck, Mrs Duck!* the farmyard animals say goodbye to their friend Mrs Duck as she waddles off on her special journey. Use funny voices to say the rhymes and perhaps act out some of the animals' actions. You could also think up some fun rhyming words of your own. Can your child count Mrs Duck's babies at the end?

Books open doors to other worlds, so take a few minutes out of your busy day to cuddle up close and lose yourselves in a story. Your child will love it – and so will you.

Jane & Clare

Jane Kemp   Clare Walters

P.S. Look out, too, for *Tiny Trumpet, Tiny Trumpet Plays Hide and Seek* and *Ten Sleepy Bunnies,* the companion books in this age range, and all the other great books in the Practical Parenting™ series.

AGE
2-3

This edition produced for The Book People Ltd, Hall Wood Avenue, Haydock, St Helens WA11 9UL

First published in Great Britain by HarperCollins*Publishers* Ltd in 2001

1 3 5 7 9 8 6 4 2

ISBN: 0-00-764678-X

Practical Parenting™ is published monthly by IPC Media.
To get Practical Parenting™ delivered to your door every month ring the subscriptions
hotline on 01444 445555 or the credit card hotline (UK orders only) on 01622 778778.

Good Luck, Mrs Duck!

Written by Jane Kemp and Clare Walters

Illustrated by Ant Parker

TED SMART

One day, Mrs Duck set off across the farmyard...

"Goodbye my dear friends, I really must go,
But soon I'll be back with TREASURE to show."

Her friends on the farm all gathered to say,
"GOOD LUCK, MRS DUCK! Take care on your way."

"So what will you do while I'm not here with you?"

"I'll wave 'til you're gone," sang Elegant Swan.

"I'll jump on this log," croaked Hoppity Frog.

"I'll make a deep bow," mooed Courteous Cow.

"I'll nibble this coat," grinned Mischievous Goat.

"I'll snooze on this mat," yawned Comfortable Cat.

"I'll hide in my house," squeaked shy Little Mouse.

"I'll bounce and I'll leap," baaed Skippety Sheep.

"I'll gallop, of course," neighed tall Handsome Horse.

"I'll dance a fine jig," oinked perky Pink Pig.

"I'll peck in my pen," clucked fluffy Brown Hen.

Mrs Duck found a place to build a warm nest,

And in it she laid five eggs of the best.

Time passed on the farm, 'til one sunny day,

"QUACK, QUACK! Look, I'm back!" they heard a voice say.

"Good morning, dear friends. It gives me great pleasure
To show you my ducklings, my fluffy gold TREASURE!"

The animals cheered, "Well done, Mrs Duck,
What beautiful babies! What perfect GOOD LUCK!"

Sharing Books From Birth to Five

AGE 0–1

- Zoo Patterns — A first focus cloth book — zebra runs
- Teddy's Toys — A touch-and-feel cloth book — Teddy's Toys
- Family Faces — A lift-the-flap board book
- Noisy Animals

AGE 1–2

- Busy Babies Go to the Gym
- Busy Babies Go Swimming
- Busy Babies Go to the Play Club
- Baby Friends Come to Play — A LIFT THE FLAP BOOK

AGE 2–3

- Ten Sleepy Bunnies — Learn to count from 1–10
- Tiny Trumpet
- Tiny Trumpet Plays Hide and Seek — A flip-the-flap book
- Good Luck, Mrs Duck!

AGE 3–5

- Rocket to the Rescue — Meet Jessie and Joe of Little Oak Farm
- The Piggy Race — Meet Jessie and Joe of Little Oak Farm
- abc — Have fun learning the alphabet!

ALL £3.99

The Practical Parenting™ books are available from all good bookshops and can be ordered direct from HarperCollins Publishers by ringing 0141 7723200 and through the HarperCollins website: www.**fire**and**water**.com

You can also order any of these titles, with free post and packaging, from the Practical Parenting™ Bookshop on 01326 569339 or send your cheque or postal order together with your name and address to: Practical Parenting™ Bookshop, Freepost, PO Box 11, Falmouth, TR10 9EN.